MYTHICAL MEALS

Making a Meal for a FAIRY

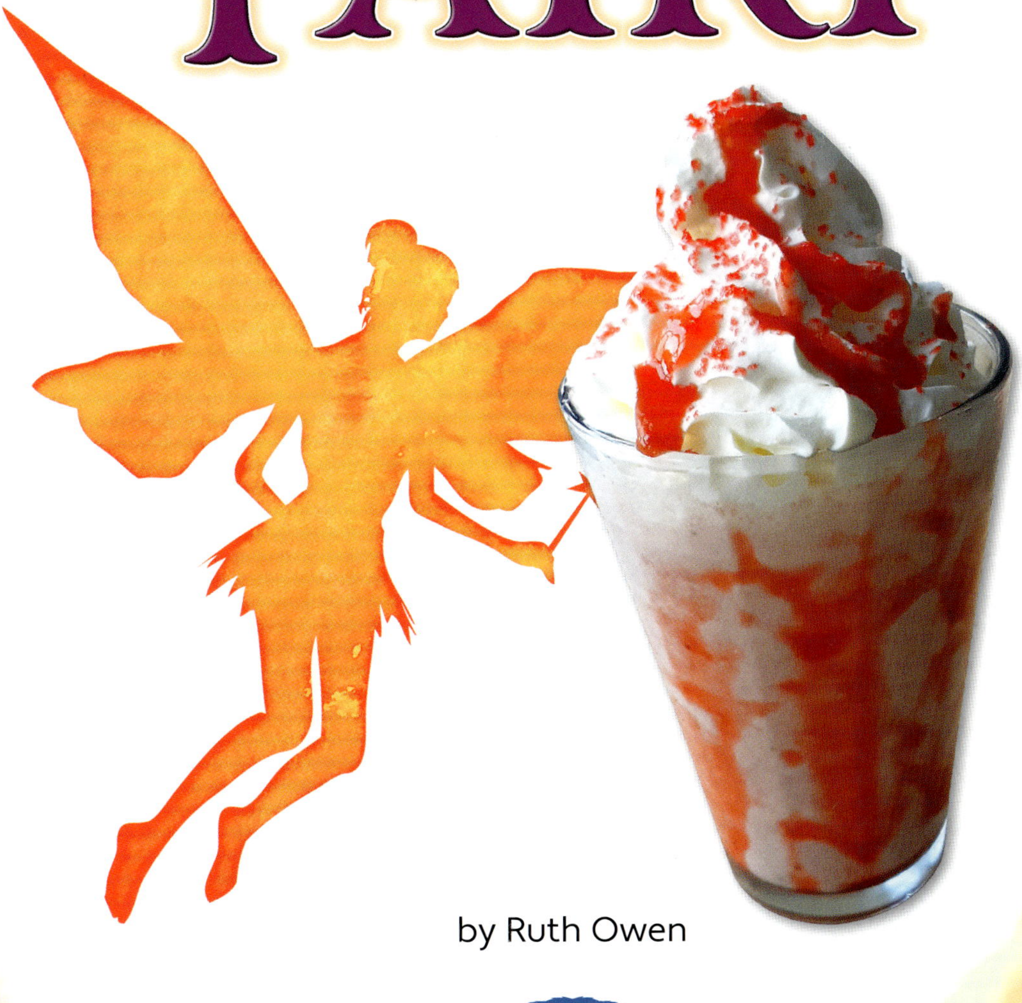

by Ruth Owen

Bearport
PUBLISHING

Minneapolis, Minnesota

CREATE!

Credits:
Cover, © Ekaterina Markelova/Shutterstock and © Shutterstock; 1, © Ruth Owen Books and © Shutterstock; 3, © Ruth Owen Books and © Shutterstock; 4, © Ruth Owen Books and © Shutterstock; 5, © Shutterstock; 6, © Ruth Owen Books and © Shutterstock; 7, © Ruth Owen Books and © Shutterstock; 8T, © Ruth Owen Books; 8B, © Shutterstock; 9, © Ruth Owen Books and © Shutterstock; 10, © Ruth Owen Books and © Shutterstock; 11, © Ruth Owen Books; 12–13, © Ruth Owen Books; 14, © Ruth Owen Books and © Shutterstock; 15, © Ruth Owen Books; 16–17, © Ruth Owen Books; 18, © Ruth Owen Books and © Shutterstock; 19, © Ruth Owen Books; 20–21, © Ruth Owen Books; 22T, © Atelier Sommerland/Shutterstock; 22B, © Science and Society/Superstock; 23L, © MShev/Shutterstock; 23R, © LFRabanedo/Shutterstock.

President: Jen Jenson
Director of Product Development: Spencer Brinker
Senior Editor: Allison Juda
Associate Editor: Charly Haley
Designer: Colin O'Dea

Library of Congress Cataloging-in-Publication Data

Names: Owen, Ruth, 1967- author.
Title: Making a meal for a fairy / by Ruth Owen.
Description: Create! books. | Minneapolis, Minnesota : Bearport Publishing Company, [2022] | Series: Mythical meals | Includes bibliographical references and index.
Identifiers: LCCN 2021006572 (print) | LCCN 2021006573 (ebook) | ISBN 9781636910673 (library binding) | ISBN 9781636910741 (ebook)
Subjects: LCSH: Cooking—Juvenile literature. | Fairies—Juvenile literature. | LCGFT: Cookbooks.
Classification: LCC TX652.5 .O9623 2022 (print) | LCC TX652.5 (ebook) | DDC 641.5/123—dc23
LC record available at https://lccn.loc.gov/2021006572
LC ebook record available at https://lccn.loc.gov/2021006573

Copyright © 2022 Bearport Publishing Company. All rights reserved. No part of this publication may be reproduced in whole or in part, stored in any retrieval system, or transmitted in any form or by any means, electronic, mechanical, photocopying, recording, or otherwise, without written permission from the publisher.

For more information, write to Bearport Publishing, 5357 Penn Avenue South, Minneapolis, MN 55419. Printed in the United States of America.

Contents

A Fairy Feast 4

Drink
Fairy Frappé 6

Appetizer
Fairy Garden Focaccia 10

Main Course
Rainbow Noodle Bowl 14

Dessert
Bite-Size Wand Cookies 18

Fairy Tales 22
Glossary.. 23
Index.. 24
Read More 24
Learn More Online 24
About the Author... 24

A Fairy Feast

A fairy is coming for dinner! Get ready to serve your tiny guest a **feast** that will remind her of her woodland home.

◄ DRINK
Sweet berries are a fairy favorite. So, welcome your new friend with a delicious strawberry **frappé**.

APPETIZER ►
Begin the meal with this tasty **focaccia** bread that's decorated with an **edible** garden.

◄ MAIN COURSE
Your fairy friend will love this noodle salad that's as colorful as she is!

DESSERT ►
For a final sweet treat, make these tiny frosted fairy wand cookies that are sprinkled with a little magic....

Get Ready to Cook!

- Always wash your hands with soap and hot water before you start cooking.
- Make sure your work surface and your cooking **equipment** are clean.
- Carefully read the recipe before you begin. If there's a step you don't understand, ask an adult for help.
- Gather all your supplies before you start.
- Carefully measure your **ingredients**. Your cooking will go better if you use the right amounts.
- When you've finished cooking, clean up the kitchen. Wash, dry, and put away your equipment.

Be Safe!

For some recipes, you'll need an adult helper. Be sure to ask for help when you use:

- Sharp objects, such as knives or scissors
- The oven, stove, or microwave
- An electric hand mixer

DRINK
Fairy Frappé

Fairies love berries. So, your little dinner guest will love this fruity frappé topped with whipped cream and a sprinkling of a little magic.

Makes 2 servings

Ingredients

- 1 tablespoon plus 1 teaspoon granulated sugar
- Food coloring of your choice
- ¼ teaspoon cornstarch
- 1 teaspoon water
- 1 ½ cups strawberries with stems removed, washed and cut into small pieces
- ¾ cup milk of your choice
- 2 tablespoons sweetened condensed milk
- 1 teaspoon vanilla extract
- 3 cups ice
- 1 can whipped cream

Equipment

- A small plate
- 2 teaspoons
- 2 small, microwavable bowls
- A small strainer
- A blender
- 2 glasses
- A dessert spoon

1 To make something magical to sprinkle on your drinks, put 1 tablespoon of sugar onto a small plate. Add 3 drops of food coloring to the sugar.

2 With a teaspoon, stir the sugar until it has all changed color. Spread the sugar out a little with the teaspoon and allow it to dry for about an hour.

3 To make the strawberry sauce, put the cornstarch and water into a microwave-safe bowl. Stir with a teaspoon until the cornstarch has **dissolved**.

4 Put 1 teaspoon of sugar and ½ cup of strawberry pieces into the bowl and stir the mixture.

5 Ask an adult helper to microwave the strawberry and cornstarch mixture for 2 minutes. Then, ask them to remove the bowl from the microwave. Allow the mixture to cool for about 10 minutes and then stir with a teaspoon.

Strained strawberry sauce

Seeds and mush

6 Next, put a small strainer over the second small bowl. Pour the strawberry sauce through the strainer. With the teaspoon, stir and press the sauce until all the liquid goes through the strainer and into the bowl, leaving just the seeds and mush behind.

7 Allow the strained strawberry sauce to cool for another 10 minutes. The sauce will thicken during this time.

8 When your colored sugar is dry and the strawberry sauce is cool, make your frappés. Put 1 cup of strawberry pieces into a blender. Add the milk, the condensed milk, the vanilla extract, and the ice to the blender.

Strawberry pieces

Milk

Condensed milk

Vanilla extract

Ice

9 Blend the ingredients together until they are smooth and creamy. This will take about 30 seconds.

10 Take one glass and hold it at a slight angle. Use a dessert spoon to **drizzle** some strawberry sauce around the inside of the glasses until you have about two spoonfuls left for decorating.

Frappé mixture

Blender

11 Pour the frappé mixture into both glasses.

12 Add whipped cream to the top of each drink. Drizzle the remaining strawberry sauce over the cream, sprinkle the top with colored sugar, and enjoy!

A MAGICAL START TO YOUR MEAL!

APPETIZER
Fairy Garden Focaccia

Fairies live among the flowers, plants, and tree roots in gardens and woodlands. Make this focaccia bread look like a secret fairy garden. Your **imagination** can run wild as you decorate it with vegetables and **herbs**.

Makes 10 servings

Ingredients

- 3 cups warm water
- 2 ½ teaspoons salt
- 3 teaspoons dried yeast
- 4 ½ cups all-purpose flour
- 1 cup olive oil
- Your choice of vegetables, herbs, and seeds for decoration. You could use cherry tomatoes, black olives, bell peppers, green onions, zucchini, red onions, basil, chives, or sesame seeds.

Equipment

- A baking pan about 16 x 12 inch (40 x 30 cm) wide and 1 in. (2.5 cm) deep
- Parchment paper
- A mixing bowl
- A wooden spoon
- A pastry brush or a wide, clean paintbrush
- A spatula
- A flat baking sheet that is at least 16 x 12 in. (40 x 30 cm)
- A clean dish towel
- Clean kitchen scissors

1. Line the baking pan with parchment paper.

2. Pour the water into the mixing bowl. Add 1 ½ teaspoons of salt to the water and stir with a wooden spoon until the salt has dissolved.

Wet, sticky dough mixture

3. Add the yeast and flour to the salt water. Stir with the wooden spoon until the mixture comes together to form a slightly runny **dough**.

4. Next, use your hands to **knead** the dough for about 5 minutes. Squash, squeeze, and stretch the dough in the bowl. It will feel very wet and sticky—almost like playing with slime!

5 Pour ½ cup of olive oil onto the parchment paper in the baking pan. Use a brush to spread it around.

6 Then, pour the dough onto the oiled parchment paper and spread it to all four sides with a spatula or your hands.

7 Pour the remaining olive oil on top of the dough and brush it evenly to cover the surface.

8 After that, completely cover the baking pan and dough with the flat baking sheet. Then, cover the baking sheet with a clean dish towel. Put the dough in a warm place to let it **rise** for 1 ½ hours.

9 After 1 ½ hours, ask an adult helper to preheat the oven to 350°F (190°C). Remove the dough from the warm place and uncover it. The dough should have doubled in size and you should see some bubbles on the surface.

10 Now it's time to make your fairy garden. Use vegetables, herbs, and seeds to get creative! Below are some ideas, but have fun making up your own.

11 When your garden is ready, sprinkle the focaccia bread with 1 teaspoon of salt.

Cherry tomatoes cut in half make this flower.

Use kitchen scissors to cut bell peppers into small pieces to make petals.

Basil leaves look like plants.

Sprinkle seeds onto the bread to look like soil.

Rings of red onion look like a flower.

Chives and green onions can be used as plant stems.

12 Ask your helper to bake the bread for 35 minutes. It is ready when the top has turned golden brown and the sides are pulling away from the pan. Time to dig into your garden!

A GARDEN THAT'S GOOD ENOUGH TO EAT!

MAIN COURSE
Rainbow Noodle Bowl

Fairy wings can be all the colors of a rainbow. Make your little friend this colorful main course of pink and purple noodles served with a rainbow of vegetables.

Makes 2 servings

Ingredients

- 2 cups salad leaves of your choice
- 4 green onions
- 1 large, thick carrot, washed and peeled
- 2 cooked beets, washed
- ½ cucumber, washed
- 2 cups water
- ¼ small red cabbage
- 2 nests thin, white noodles (rice, glass, or similar)
- 1 lemon
- Your choice salad ingredients
- Your choice salad dressing

Equipment

- 2 shallow bowls
- Clean kitchen scissors
- Small cookie cutters in shapes such as flowers, butterflies, and stars
- A pot
- Metal tongs
- A pot holder
- A colander

1 Begin by preparing your salad ingredients. Take the two bowls and put salad leaves in the bottom of each.

2 Use scissors to carefully cut off the root ends of the green onions. Then, cut each onion into pieces about ½ in. (1.25 cm) long. Set aside the onion pieces.

3 Ask an adult helper to cut the carrot and beets into slices that are about ¼ in. (0.6 cm) thick. Then, use cookie cutters to cut shapes from the slices. Set aside.

4 Ask your helper to cut the cucumber into slices about ¼ in. (0.6 cm) thick. Use scissors to carefully cut five tiny triangles from the edge of each slice to make them look like flowers. Put the cucumber flowers to the side.

Red cabbage

5. To prepare the noodles, put 2 cups of water into a pot. Ask your adult helper to cut the red cabbage into about 5 pieces and put them into the water.

6. Ask your helper to heat the water on the stove. Once the water is boiling, allow the water and cabbage to boil for 5 minutes. Then ask your helper to take the pot off the stove and place it on a pot holder. Using metal tongs, remove the cabbage from the water.

Noodles

7. Next, use the metal tongs to carefully put the noodles into the colorful water. Leave the noodles to soak for 10 minutes, or until they have turned purple.

> The water will look very dark but the noodles will be a bright purple color.

8. Place a colander in the sink. Ask your adult helper to set the pot near the colander. With the tongs, carefully remove the noodles from the water and place them into the colander. Gently shake the colander over the sink to remove as much water as possible from the noodles.

9 Use the tongs to put half of the noodles into each bowl, on top of the salad leaves.

10 Ask your adult helper to cut a lemon in half. Squeeze the juice from one half over the noodles in one of the bowls. Where the lemon juice touches the purple noodles, they will turn pink! Repeat with the second bowl.

11 Decorate each bowl with the carrot, beet, and cucumber shapes. Add any other ingredients you'd like.

12 Finally, sprinkle half of the chopped green onions on top of each bowl and drizzle with the dressing. Enjoy!

CRUNCHY, CUTE, AND COLORFUL!

DESSERT
Bite-Size Wand Cookies

A fairy can cast spells and make wishes come true. But to do her magic, she needs a wand! Finish your dinner with these fairy-sized, mini cookies that look just like your friend's magic wand.

Makes 10 servings

Ingredients

- 1 stick butter, softened
- ¼ cup granulated sugar
- 1 egg
- 1 teaspoon vanilla extract
- ¼ teaspoon baking powder
- 1 ½ cups plus 1 tablespoon all-purpose flour
- 1 cup powdered sugar
- 4 teaspoons water
- 5 different food colorings in your choice of colors
- Sprinkles

Equipment

- 50 wooden toothpicks
- 6 small bowls
- A mixing bowl
- An electric hand mixer
- A wooden spoon
- Parchment paper
- A rolling pin
- A star-shaped cookie cutter about 1 in. (2.5 cm) wide
- 2 baking sheets
- 5 teaspoons
- A small, clean paintbrush

Always remove the toothpick before you bite into your cookie.

1. Ask an adult helper to preheat the oven to 350°F (175°C). Put the toothpicks in a small bowl of water to soak. This will keep them from burning in the oven.

2. Put the butter and granulated sugar into a mixing bowl. Use an electric mixer to **beat** the butter and sugar together until it looks pale and creamy.

3. Add the egg and vanilla extract to the bowl and beat until all the ingredients are well mixed.

4. Add the baking powder to the bowl. Then, add 1 ½ cups flour a little at a time, stirring with a wooden spoon. When the mixture is thick, use your hands to squeeze it into a ball of dough.

5 Wrap the dough in parchment paper and place in the refrigerator for 30 minutes to chill.

> Chilling the dough makes it easier to roll out.

6 **Dust** your work surface with 1 tablespoon of flour. Use a rolling pin to roll out the dough until it's about ¼ in. (0.6 cm) thick.

7 Use a cookie cutter to stamp the dough. Take a toothpick from the bowl, and shake off any extra water. Then, carefully push the toothpick about ½ in. (1.25 cm) into the side of the cookie. Place the cookie on a baking sheet. Continue to cut stars from the dough. Give each star a toothpick handle and place it onto the baking sheet.

8 Squeeze the leftover dough into a ball and roll it out again. Then, continue to cut star cookies, add toothpicks, and place them on the baking sheet. Continue until you have used all of the dough.

9 Ask your adult helper to bake the cookies for 10 minutes. Then, ask your helper to remove them from the oven and allow to cool completely.

10 To make the frosting, put the powdered sugar and water into a small bowl. Mix with a teaspoon until the frosting is thick and smooth.

11 Divide the frosting among the other 4 small bowls. Add 1 drop of food coloring to a bowl and mix with a teaspoon. Repeat with the other bowls, adding a different color to each and mixing with a different teaspoon.

> If you want the frosting to be a brighter color, add another drop of coloring.

12 Using a small paint brush, paint one side of each cookie with frosting. Be sure to rinse and dry your brush between colors. Then, while the frosting is still wet, decorate the tiny cookies with your choice of sprinkles.

CAST A SPELL WITH THIS SWEET TREAT!

Fairy Tales

Get to know more about your dinner guest by checking out these fun **myths** and facts about fairies.

People around the world have told stories of fairies for hundreds of years. Many fairies are said to look like tiny humans. They often live in gardens and woodlands.

Some fairies help us. They can blow away worries or take care of sick animals. And—of course—some fairies collect our baby teeth that have fallen out and leave behind gifts.

Frances Griffiths with the cardboard fairies

In 1917, two young cousins said they had photographed fairies in a garden. The five photos taken by Frances Griffiths and Elsie Wright caused a lot of excitement. Many years later, Frances and Elsie admitted that the fairies were actually cardboard cutouts.

IF YOU WERE HAVING DINNER WITH A FAIRY, WHAT WOULD YOU LIKE TO ASK HER?

Glossary

beat to mix ingredients until they are smooth using a spoon, fork, whisk, or electric mixer

dissolved completely mixed into a liquid

dough a mixture of flour, water, and other ingredients that is used to make pasta, bread, or cookies

drizzle to trickle a liquid over something

dust to sprinkle with flour to keep dough from sticking

edible able to be eaten

equipment tools or items that are used to do a job

feast a large meal with lots of different dishes

focaccia a flat bread that is made in Italy

frappé a sweet drink made with ice

herbs plants that are used for flavoring food

imagination the ability to think up ideas and think creatively

ingredients the things that are used to make food

knead to squeeze dough with your hands many times

myths old stories that tell of strange or magical events and creatures

rise to puff up and grow bigger

23

Index

focaccia 4, 10, 13
gardens 4, 10, 13, 22
Griffiths, Frances 22
myths 22
safety 5
wands 4, 18
wings 14
woodlands 4, 10, 22
Wright, Elsie 22

Read More

Chambers, Catherine. *The Tooth Fairy (Autobiographies You Never Thought You'd Read).* Chicago: Heinemann-Raintree, 2016.

Williams, Sam. *Fairy Puzzles (Magical Puzzles).* New York: Windmill Books, 2020.

Learn More Online

1. Go to **www.factsurfer.com**
2. Enter **"Fairy Meals"** into the search box.
3. Click on the cover of this book to see a list of websites.

About the Author

Ruth Owen has been developing and writing children's books for more than 10 years. She lives in Cornwall, England, just minutes from the ocean. Ruth loves cooking and making up recipes. Her favorite dish in this book is the fairy garden focaccia bread. Making this bread is like painting with vegetables!